S ^   1 GARLAND is a much-loved author-illustrator
~ 10 has published over 40 books for children.
evious titles for Frances Lincoln are *Dashing Dog*,
vas written by Margaret Mahy, and *Eddie's Garden*.
1h comes from a family of writers, and trained
ypographer at the London College of Printing.
1e has four children and two grandchildren,
and lives in the Cotswolds.

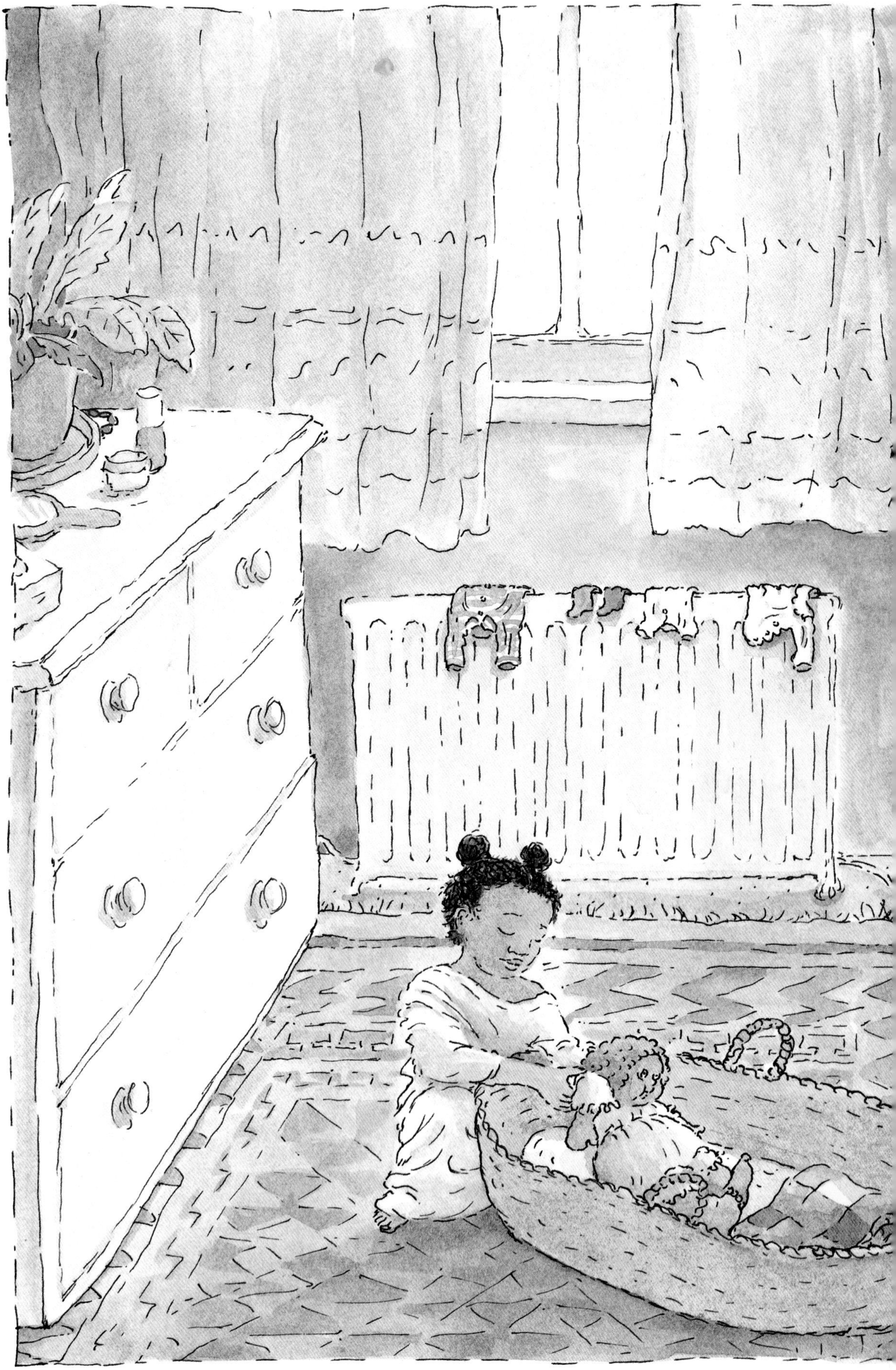

With love to
Gillian and Pearl

Billy and Belle copyright © Frances Lincoln Limited 2004
Text and illustrations copyright © Sarah Garland 1992

First published in the United Kingdom in 1992 by Reinhardt Books,
in association with Viking, Penguin Group.

This edition first published in 2004 by Frances Lincoln Children's Books,
4 Torriano Mews, Torriano Avenue, London, NW5 2RZ

Distributed in the USA by Publishers Group West

www.franceslincoln.com

British Library Cataloguing in Publication Data available on request

ISBN 1-84507-038-0

Printed in Singapore

3 5 7 9 8 6 4 2

Billy and Belle

zzzzzz

Sarah Garland

FRANCES LINCOLN CHILDREN'S BOOKS

On Monday morning Billy lay
in bed for a long time.

He was thinking about his hamster,
and about the baby that would soon be born.

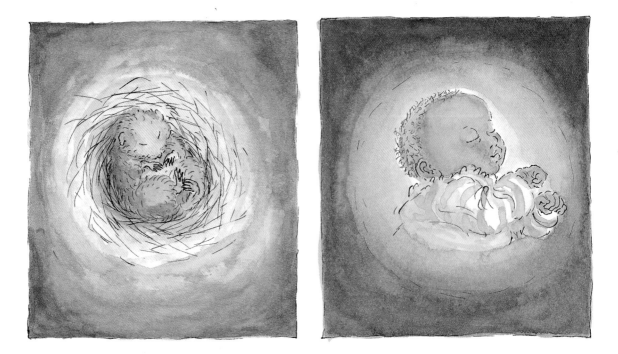

He heard Dad filling the kettle.
He heard Mum dressing Belle.

He heard Spot barking.
He smelt toast burning.

He was late for breakfast.

Billy got ready for school.

Today, Belle was coming too

because Mum and Dad were going
to the hospital.

Billy and Belle were going to school with
their neighbour, Mrs Plum.

Belle was very excited.

Mrs Plum left them with the teacher.

Billy showed his hamster to his friends.

Everyone had brought a pet.

John had a tortoise.

Pat had a rat.

Rita had a frog.

Donna had
a guinea pig.

Hassan had
a caterpillar.

Kelly had
a mouse.

Dino had a beetle.

Sam had a snail.

Alan had a gerbil.

Anna had a rabbit.

Billy had a hamster.

And Belle had a spider.

The teacher looked at the spider,

then she put the pets out in the playground.

She asked the class to draw their pets.

Belle tried to remember how many legs
her spider had, but she couldn't... so...

she went quietly outside

to look for her spider.

She looked and looked…

and looked, until at last

she found it

on her jumper.

But when everyone came out at playtime...

Oh no! All the pets had escaped!

High and low, they hunted for their pets...

until they found them all at last.

When the class had settled down again,

Who will tell us about their pet and show us their picture?

Billy showed his picture.

Hamsters are nocturnal. That means they are awake all night and asleep all day.

My turn now, Miss!

At three o' clock pet day was over.

Dad told Billy and Belle the good news.

They talked about the baby,

and ate their tea,

and got ready for bed.

Billy lay in bed, thinking about the baby.

He heard a cab stop outside.
He heard Dad running up the stairs.

Billy! Belle! Mum is home with Adam!

Then Billy and Belle saw their new baby brother for the first time.

And Billy's hamster woke up.

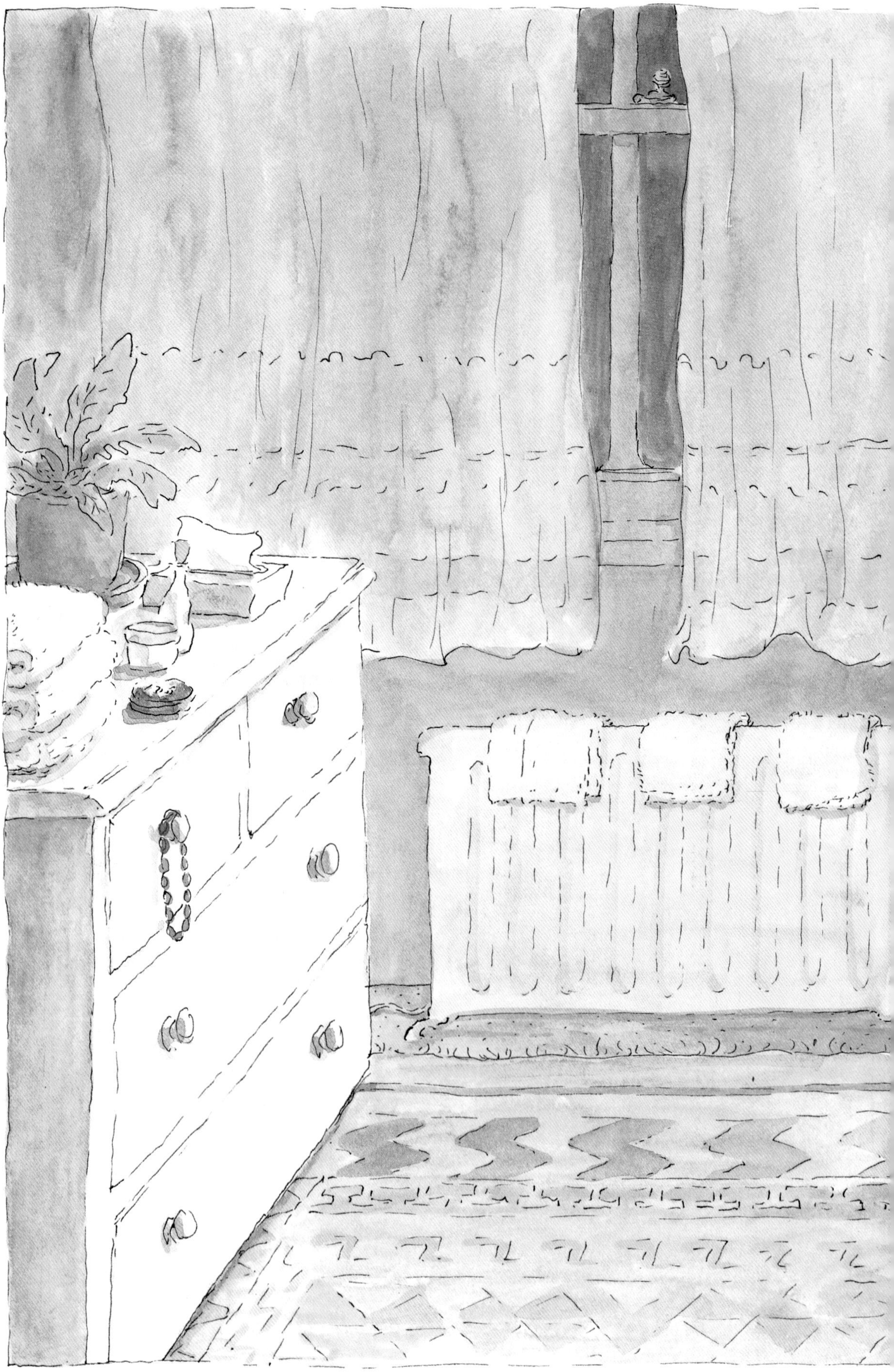

MORE TITLES FROM
FRANCES LINCOLN CHILDREN'S BOOKS

EDDIE'S GARDEN
Sarah Garland

What makes Eddie's garden grow? Earth, rain, warm sun, and all sorts
of creatures! Eddie works hard in his garden – digging, pulling up the
weeds and watering his plants. Soon the garden looks wonderful, from
Eddie's bean den to his tall sunflowers, and it's full of tasty treats that
will make his picnic with Lily, Mum and Grandad the best one ever!
ISBN 1-84507-015-1

DASHING DOG
Margaret Mahy
Illustrated by Sarah Garland

Follow the chaotic antics of the dashing dog and his family in a mad,
dizzy and joyful walk along the beach… With Margaret Mahy's wildly
funny sense of humour and Sarah Garland's exuberant illustrations,
this is a picture book made in heaven.
ISBN 0-7112-1977-X

ONE ROUND MOON AND A STAR FOR ME
Ingrid Mennen
Illustrated by Niki Daly

A young African boy watches a shooting star falling for his mama's new
baby. The whole village comes together to provide gifts for mother and
child. But when he sees his papa smiling at the baby's tiny hands which
are just like Papa's own hands, the boy's heart grows dark, like a night
with no moon. At last he asks, "Papa, are you really my papa too?"
ISBN 1-84507-024-0

Frances Lincoln titles are available from all good bookshops.
You can also buy books and find out more about your favourite titles,
authors and illustrators on our website: www.franceslincoln.com